When Freedom Comes

Hope's Revolutionary War Diary

· Book Three ·

by Kristiana Gregory

Scholastic Inc. New York

Philadelphia
1777

Thursday, the 25th of December, 1777

'Tis Christmas afternoon, but it does not feel like it — enemy soldiers still live in our home! For three months they have been here telling us how to cook their dumplings and beef and making us serve them English tea (this we refuse to drink). How much longer must I curtsy to these men in dirty red coats?

I am writing by the pale light of our parlor window while Mother rocks baby Faith for a nap. In the wee hours this morning — 'twas three o'clock — we awoke when Major Quigley and his men burst through the front door singing. We could smell rum and onions from their wild night out. They stomped upstairs, as if this were a tavern and not our quiet little house.

"Never mind, Hope," Mama whispered when I sat up. "Go back to sleep." She and Miss Sarah share a bed, and Faith and I are on the trundle.

Our cat stayed curled by my feet, purring as if all were well! I lay wide-awake until a snowy light filled our window. In the kitchen, I dressed Faith by the warm hearth while Ethan brought in wood from the yard. Soon our fire was blazing and my brother said, "Time for presents!"

Mama and I looked at each other. We had forgotten 'twas Christmas!

Oh, dear, noise from the attic. The soldiers are stirring and will soon demand something to eat.

Christmas evening

Faith and I are in Mama's room. The door is ajar so we can see into the parlor where Major Quigley sits by the fire with four men. His powdered wig has a black satin bow at the end of its pigtail. The wig is full of fleas. This I know because he keeps scratching his scalp with the stem of his pipe. Also, I have stood inches away from him and have seen the bugs hopping along his neck.

As I write this by a short candle, Faith is on the trundle playing with the blocks our brother made her. She is almost one year and six months, with red curls just falling out of her mobcap.

But about today . . . Ethan surprised us each with a gift. He is apprenticed down at the wharf with one of the ship builders, so from scraps of wood he was able to make toy blocks.

The corners are sanded smooth and on each side he painted a letter, to help Faith learn her ABCs when she is a bit older.

To Mother he gave a small flag, the Stars and Stripes. He found it in a trash heap where a British warship is docked. He dusted it off then hid it in his sleeve. Now she has it safe inside her pillow. We do not want Major Quigley to take it away.

Miss Sarah is our dear friend from next door who is living with us until her husband, Mr. Dean, returns from the war. Ethan gave her a silver button he found in the street, polished and pretty. We think it dropped off an officer's cloak. She is going to make it into a brooch.

And to me, my dear brother gave this small journal.

My flame is low . . . shall tell of it tomorrow . . .

Thursday, the 1st of January, 1778

Outside, the mercury stands at six degrees. Our thermometer is nailed to the wall by our back door.

A week has passed since Christmas and now 'tis a new year, 1778. Wind spits falling snow against our windows. We cannot look out until we scratch away the inside ice. From the small table where I sit, I can see that our street is white and three Redcoats are passing by with bayonets on their shoulders. Snow comes up to the shins of their tall black boots.

Today a great commotion drew most of us from our homes. Ten teams of oxen left Philadelphia, driven by women! They are heading for Valley Forge to deliver supplies to General Washington's starving army. 'Tis where Papa and Mr. Dean are, about eighteen miles away. Along with food these women are taking two thousand shirts. Two thousand!

Mama said many of these shirts were sewn by American girls who embroidered their names inside, by the collar. These are called Bounty Shirts. The young ladies hope that when the war ends, soldiers will return to thank them and mayhap marry them, too.

I pray the British do not use their guns to stop these wagons of mercy. Also, I pray Papa and Mr. Dean do not get a Bounty Shirt! They already have us waiting for them.

Now, about Ethan's gift to me, this journal. 'Tis made of coarse brown paper and sewn together with red thread. On the front cover it says LOG. He found this in the trash as well. It had belonged to a ship's captain, so my brother tore out the pages that had words and numbers written on them. He is clever for fifteen.

When Mama and I told him we were sorry

to have planned no Christmas gifts, he laughed and picked Faith up from the floor.

"I have ye," he said, "and a dry roof."

Ethan did not say so but I know he was remembering his terrible months in the British gaol, where he was in prison. He still limps from the whipping to his bare feet.

Friday, the 2nd of January

My eleventh birthday! Mama baked a small square cake with a sprinkling of sugar on top. I was so pleased to sit at supper with Faith on my lap and the others around the table. Miss Sarah is going to have a baby, but you can hardly tell. She just looks plump.

I was thankful that Major Quigley and his men had left us alone for another night out on the town. I want this war to be over and Papa to return. Am I selfish to also want my locket back? Inside is a drawing of Papa and a lock of his brown hair. Some months ago, a British officer ripped it off my neck in the marketplace. I am still angry about this. Now that the officer has learned what my father looks like, Papa must stay away. The Redcoats know he was with the Sons of Liberty and killed some of their men.

For this, they cut off Papa's left hand with a sword.

Monday, the 5th of January

More snow.

After our bread was baking and a flurry of customers came, I walked to the dressmaker's shoppe. The kind lady shook her head at me. She could not speak because of soldiers sitting by her fire. But her eyes told me that Polly Adams had not been by.

My friend and I have been secretly writing notes to each other then leaving them with the dressmaker for safekeeping. Our mothers forbid us to see each other because we — the Potter family — are Patriots. Polly's parents are Loyalists. Anyone loyal to King George is an enemy, Mama says.

This war is hard on our friendship.

Along with my letter to Polly, I gave the dressmaker a small basket of cinnamon apple tarts baked this morning. She smiled at me with sad eyes and tucked a loose strand of hair under her cap. I could tell the soldiers had just come in from the snow, because the wool of their red coats stunk in the warm room.

Another day

I worry about Polly. This afternoon I put on my cloak and cap, then walked by her house.

Though her window was frosty, I was able to see a fire glowing in her hearth and her two little brothers chasing each other around the table. Polly's father is a baker like Papa and Hannie. We all live on Bread Street. Our only neighbor who does not cook anything to sell is Mr. Walker, the wig maker.

At Hannie's, I rapped on the door. Mayhap she could give me news about my friend. She invited me in — cheerful as usual — but before I could ask questions, my eyes fell on a shocking sight.

A British soldier was paying Hannie silver coins for the platter of pastries she held.

Hannie was doing business with our enemy!

'Tis true, she and her husband have five small children to feed, and she is in the same plump condition as Miss Sarah. But still . . . how could she?

Before bed

I have not told Mama about Hannie. And who can I ask about Polly? Is she ill? Or mayhap she has turned her own heart toward King George and now hates me. I cannot forget that her mother once called me a "rebel." She whispered the word as if it were poison.

Saturday, the 24th of January

Mama has kept me home from school for weeks. She feels safer with me here, but she also needs my help. With Papa gone and Ethan at the shipyard, Miss Sarah and I rise early with her to get all our baking done. Every day save Sunday. Even on the coldest mornings I walk to the marketplace with my basket of "Potter's Pies."

"One penny!" I call out in the cold air, as my fingers grow numb. "Tarts, one penny!"

With no school I miss seeing Polly. Though we are not allowed to speak to each other, in school we at least could secretly smile at each other. We knew we were still friends.

It feels good helping Mother, but I know not what I will do if a Redcoat stops me. If he wants to give me a penny for a tart, will I sell to him?

Mercury, fourteen degrees in the sunshine.

Monday, the 26th of January

Twice a week I go to Hannie's with one of Mother's fresh fruit pies. In trade, she gives us a round loaf of rye bread or wheat. Today her house was crowded with relatives visiting from Valley Forge. They want Hannie and her family to leave Philadelphia and come stay with them, away from the British. Also visiting are her niece, Abigail, and a friend, Lucy. They are eleven years old, as am I!

Oh, how happy I was to finally chit and chat with girls my age, for 'tis been such a long time without my Polly. Though they are from the country and I the city, our dresses were much the same — blue and white cotton with a plain ruffle at our sleeve, our aprons covering the front of our skirts. Even our mobcaps look as if one mother made all three. But I became uneasy when they spoke of our American soldiers, who are camped in the snow near their farmhouses. Lucy said most of the men are dressed in rags with no shoes. Many are dying from hunger and cold and illness. The other day two deserters were hanged from a tree after they were caught running away from camp.

At Lucy's words, my heart froze with fear. What about Papa and Mr. Dean? Are they ill and hungry? Will their courage fail them? Would they try to desert?

Before bed

After we washed the supper plates and stacked them in the cupboard, Mama sat at the table to write Papa a letter. She let me sign my name next to hers with three X's to mark my kisses. We will ask Hannie's relatives to carry it when they return to Valley Forge.

We worry about Papa, remembering that when he marched away the stump of his lost hand was still oozing. It had not yet healed.

Tonight, when we opened the front door to sweep out the crumbs, Faith toddled into the street. Ethan caught her by the back of her shirt, just as a horseman rode by at a gallop. Another inch and she would have been trampled. Mother smacked her bottom and sat her down on our little stool by the stove. Oh, how Faith cried and cried, but she must learn her lesson somehow.

With the British living in our city, so many rules are being broken. It is customary that gentlemen walk their horses through the streets, not ride. 'Tis much safer. But now we must take greater caution with Faith.

Tuesday, the 27th of January

At noon I took our letter to Hannie's. Abigail's father said he will deliver it to Washington's camp himself. How I wish Abigail and Lucy could stay longer. Only now do I admit how lonely am I.

Evening, half past seven

This afternoon Mama sent me to Mr. Walker's to invite him for supper. He lives by himself with his many wigs, but he is a kindly gentleman.

Before stepping into his shoppe, I peeked through his window. Lucy was inside, sitting in front of a looking glass. Mr. Walker stood behind her with scissors. Before my eyes, he cut off her beautiful long tresses. So shocked was I, I could not open the door.

When Lucy's shorn hair was coiled neatly inside a box, she tied on her cap and held out her hand. Mr. Walker dropped nine shillings into her palm.

I hurried away from his shoppe with one thought: What if Lucy's hair should now be woven into a wig for an Englishman?

Mama greeted me while tying on a clean

apron. "Well?" said she. "Is the good fellow coming?"

I took a deep breath. I did not want to lie, nor did I want to say what had happened.

"Mr. Walker was with a customer," said I. "In half an hour I shall return to ask him."

Saturday, the 31st of January

Children are skating on the river. The Delaware is a short walk from our house, so I took Faith, holding her hand the whole way. I did not want her to be trampled by an Englishman on horseback. Faith's woolen leggings were so thick under her little dress and cloak that she waddled like a duck.

When I saw Polly on the ice, I wanted to run to my friend. After some moments she looked up. Her smile surprised me and warmed my heart. Then she glanced at her mother, who was standing on the dock. With her hands, Polly pretended she was ripping a piece of paper, then nodded toward her mother.

I understood what she was trying to tell me. It seems her mother found my note to her and tore it up. Mayhap Polly is now forbidden to write. That would explain why the dressmaker had no letter for me.

There must be another way for us to stay friends!

Often I think about Polly, but 'tis always on my mind that the soldiers at Valley Forge — Papa and Mr. Dean — are suffering from cold and hunger.

Another thought

As long as the Redcoats are in our house, I do not let them see me writing in this journal. They might take it away from me, just to laugh at a girl's private thoughts. Now, to return it to its hiding place, under the trundle . . . it fits between the ropes so Faith and I do not feel its lump.

Sunday, the 15th of February

Have not written for a fortnight. 'Tis not I who has been sick this time, but Major Quigley and three of his men. We have been up the stairs and down the stairs too many times to count, trying to ease their bad colds. Hot broth and plumped up pillows is the best we can do. I said naught, but methinks they should return to England and rest in their own feather beds with their own daughters tending them.

The attic — which had been my special room — is a mess with their clothes and booty strewn about. Their quilts and linens of course were stolen from our friends who fled the city.

I even saw the Major wearing a yellow waistcoat with black buttons and a silk neck scarf that had belonged to our neighbor Mr. Krenberry.

Then yesterday I saw among their things Mrs. Krenberry's china teapot. 'Tis a beautiful pale blue with tiny red flowers. I remember it from when Mother and I sat at her table for tea. Methinks that her lovely cups and saucers were broken during the thievery. The Krenberrys shall be sad to learn how much has been taken from them.

Mercury, twenty-seven degrees.

Later

We went to services this morning at Christ Church and sat in our usual pew. I am still thinking about the men who were in the row across from us.

Hessian soldiers! They whispered to one another in German whilst looking up songs in the hymnals. Their swords lay on the floor by their feet. Some pretty German girls from another part of Pennsylvania were sitting behind them, giggling. Twice the rector cleared his throat and looked at the girls with a frown.

Do our enemies worship the same God as we do? How can this be? Surely they pray that King George will win this war, but we Patriots are praying that we will win. Who does God listen to?

Tuesday, the 17th of February

Mother and I are in distress.

The tinsmith from Chestnut Street came to our door with a message from Valley Forge. He would not say how word came his way, only this:

"Mrs. Potter, your husband received your letter and sends his regards. Do not be alarmed, Madam, but he suffers from weak lungs and fits of coughing, pneumonia it is believed." The tinsmith stamped his feet from the cold, blowing on his reddened fingers. Mama invited him to warm himself by our fire, but he turned to leave.

"Please, sir," said Mama. "At least let us give thee something for thy family." She handed the man a hot beef pie wrapped in a cloth, thanked him again, then closed the door.

When she turned to me, her eyes were wet.

"Hope, we must do something for thy father."

"Let us go to Valley Forge," said I. "We can stay with Auntie and Uncle whilst we nurse Papa."

Mother looked up at the ceiling. A sprinkling of dust from a knothole in one of the planks fell down upon our table. The soldiers upstairs must have been moving something across the floor.

"'Tis a good idea, daughter," she said. But Mama was quiet for the rest of the evening.

Next morning

Windy, no sun. It seems the sky rises up to heaven like a gray curtain. There are no clouds or shadows. Ice along the street makes it slippery to walk, so I am careful when I go outside.

I have not found a way to get past Polly's mother — to speak to my friend or to see her. 'Tis unfair that we must be kept apart. I believe in my soul that Polly is a Patriot, but she must obey her parents.

Mother and Miss Sarah are discussing Valley Forge. One idea is that Mama and I could go together and leave Faith here with Miss Sarah. But the soldiers are mean. Who knows what they would do with a tiny girl and a woman about to have a baby. Ethan might be able to protect them, but he has a temper. Mother worries he would say something rash to the Redcoats, which could bring more trouble.

And if we all go to Valley Forge, Major Quigley would be here alone to abuse our house. It happened next door to Miss Sarah's lovely home and also to other friends' homes in the neighborhood. Yesterday, the wooden fence in our garden was chopped up and carted off by Redcoats. Firewood for the king's army, they said. These soldiers also knocked down our privy and tore off the door to use for kindling.

Mama's hands were shaking, she was so angry, and her face was red. I bade her come in, not to watch.

"Pigs," she said under her breath as she sat in her chair.

Ethan spent half the day setting the privy right again. Now that there is no door, he hung one of Mother's tablecloths over the opening for privacy.

Alas, we are afraid to leave Philadelphia as long as the British think they can take what they want. Papa himself would say we must stay here to protect our home.

Every hour that passes, I worry about my father. Mayhap his wound is infected and that is why he is ill.

We must hurry!

Noon

Mother is still thinking about Valley Forge. She prays on her knees by the side of her bed, her hands folded toward heaven. Her quiet tears make me heartsore.

Four o'clock in the afternoon

Must write quickly. Mother is serving tea to Major Quigley in the parlor, with shortbread we baked this morning. She is using Mrs. Krenberry's teapot! Mama's plan is to rescue it for her friend. Just an hour ago she told the Major that ours had sprung a leak. As we did not want them to be without their afternoon tea, could we please borrow theirs? They agreed!

We have a secret . . . before dawn on the morrow, Ethan shall set out for Valley Forge. If he walks briskly and is not stopped by soldiers, he should arrive by nightfall. He'll carry only a meat sandwich, some figs, and an apple wrapped in his handkerchief. No papers or letter. His story — if he is stopped — is that he is visiting his sweetheart in the valley.

'Twill be my brother Ethan who shall nurse Papa and bring him home as soon as possible. He will also look after Mr. Dean's well-being.

And Mother, Miss Sarah, and I will be here to guard our house.

Friday, the 20th of February

I have lost interest in my sampler. Along the borders I have sewn red cross-stitches with a white star in each corner. So far, with blue thread, I have only spelled out "Let not mercy and Truth forsake thee:" Methinks 'tis pretty, but Mama says half a job done is no job done at all. The rest of the proverb is "... bind Them about thy neck; write Them upon the tablet of thine heart." It will take weeks for me to embroider those words.

Tuesday, the 24th of February

We await word from Ethan, though he has been gone just six days.

Mama keeps busy with all our baking, our customers, and waiting on Major Quigley. He noticed Ethan was not here.

"Where is that lad of yours?" he asked in a gruff manner. He leaned back in his chair, then stretched his legs by putting his feet upon the table. A spoon rattled in a saucer. My mother eyed his dirty boots, but he did not remove them.

"My son is spending more time at the shipyard," she said. "He is here in the evenings when thou and thy brutes are at the taverns, then he leaves again in the morn. People with honest work get out of bed before noon, Major."

He narrowed his eyes at Mama. "Someday, Madam, you will regret your words."

"Sir," she said, "someday I shall rejoice that ye are no longer under my roof."

I was stunned to hear my mother speak so boldly. Major Quigley stared at her with a trembling chin. Methinks he would have struck her had I not come to her side.

Another thing, I could not believe she had lied — my mother, of all people. She and Papa have always insisted I tell the truth, no matter what.

Later, when I asked why she made up a story, she went to a window and scratched at the ice until there was a large enough space to look out. Redcoats were gathered in the street around a fire, warming their hands.

"'Tis war, Hope. We must protect our family. If the Major knows Ethan is with

General Washington's army, he could make trouble for us."

Saturday, the 28th of February

'Tis the first wedding anniversary of Miss Sarah and Mr. Dean. Her apron no longer fits around her waist, she is so big. Mama gave her a sheet folded lengthwise, which she can wear over her dress. 'Tis fastened behind her back, pinned by the brooch she made from Ethan's button. The baby should come in April, Mama thinks.

Before bed

A miracle has happened in Valley Forge. No, 'tis not word from Ethan, but news brought in by couriers on horseback — something wonderful for all.

Yesterday soldiers discovered the Schuylkill River flowing with shad. Though ice was thick along the banks, they were able to catch hundreds upon hundreds with nets.

Miss Sarah said this means the famine is over. "For an icy river to overflow with fish in the middle of winter" — she spoke with tears — "'tis unheard of, a sign God is watching over our men."

Mama agreed. "I have not seen such a thing in my lifetime," she said.

In our cellar we have jars of shad that we pickled last summer. We bought them at market from some fishermen. They stink (the fish), but taste good atop a piece of salted bread. Mayhap Papa will eat some of the shad caught yesterday and feel better because he shall be reminded of home.

Mercury, twenty-nine degrees in the sunshine.

Thursday, the 5th of March

Gales of wind today. The curtain on our privy flew up to its little roof and stuck there. When Mama climbed up to get it, the lacy cloth flew out of her hands and down the street and sailed over the roof of the bookshoppe like a big white kite. So now we have no door at all. Miss Sarah and Mama and I must take turns standing guard while one of us uses the privy. 'Tis cold out there, but far better than what the Redcoats are doing to Miss Sarah's house.

A boy delivering newspapers told us the soldiers living there cut a hole in the parlor floor and do their business right there. The stink falls into her lovely stone cellar. Miss Sarah dares not think about how much this upsets her, for there is naught any of us can do.

Evening

Because of fierce winds, several British ships were blown from their moorings and smashed against the docks. Before the Redcoats knew what to do, a newly built brig and a man-o'-war were sunk. Hooray, I say.

Now our cat is plump, too, like Miss Sarah and Hannie. Mama says that soon there shall be kittens. In the corner of our room I have made a cozy bed for her from one of my old aprons. I do not want the soldiers to bother our kitty when she needs to be alone.

My Chubby Strawberry — that is, Faith — said my name today. It sounds like "Bope." She is such a funny little sister, calling me through the house. "Bope . . . Bope!" She cannot say her H's.

Sunday, the 8th of March

At long last, the snow and ice have melted. I walked to church without my cloak, just a shawl over my shoulders. Though the sun feels warm, there is a breeze off the river. Faith wore a knit smock with a high collar. Her hair is growing, and now it curls to her chin. Methinks she looks like a real little girl and no longer a baby.

The Hessians were in the same row as last time. Before the Redcoats captured our city, General Washington would sit in the pew near us whenever he was able to visit Philadelphia. I can still see him in my mind, his fine bearing and devotion.

I do not understand the German language, but one of our neighbors does. After services he told us that the Hessians had been talking about the next battle. The British plan to march into Valley Forge with cannons, bayonets, and muskets.

"They will destroy the American troops," our neighbor said. "Every last one."

Mother turned pale. We hurried home.

Now, 'tis time to help Mama put supper on the table. I can hear rain pattering against the windows.

Evening, nine o'clock

The house is quiet at last, and dark. Only red coals in our hearth remain and this last bit of candle by which I write. My hand casts such a shadow on this page, 'tis hard for me to see my words.

Mama and Miss Sarah are asleep. Faith is watching me from the trundle.

"Close your eyes," I whisper to her. "I shall come to bed in a moment."

When I crawl under our quilt I shall tell her that angels are watching over her while she sleeps, and that tomorrow will be a beautiful day. I shall not tell my sister what the Redcoats plan to do, nor how worried I am for our Papa.

Tuesday, the 17th of March

'Tis hard to believe, but deserters from Washington's army arrive in Philadelphia nearly every day! Today we saw three of them by the docks, proud they had escaped the guards at Valley Forge. They wore shamrocks in their hats because 'tis Saint Patrick's Day.

"Cowards," Mama said to them when they passed our corner. "Ye should be hanged."

Alas, they shan't be shot or hanged, but instead given passage to England on the next ship to sail out. The British General Howe says they will find a hero's welcome when they land. At least this is what the neighbors are saying.

Miss Sarah and Mama are outraged, but do not speak of it lest Major Quigley hears. But in bed, I listen to their whispers.

"Fie on those men for calling themselves Americans," said Mother.

"Traitors," said Miss Sarah. "We shall see whose side they are on after we win this war."

I wish I could talk to Mama about Polly, but I know how she feels about Mr. and Mrs. Adams.

"Turncoats," she had called them when she saw Polly's parents cheer the king's army.

Someone who wears a coat then turns it inside out to fool an enemy is worse than a coward, she and Papa told me. They are traitors to the noble cause of liberty.

My heart is heavy, missing Polly.

Friday, the 20th of March

A robin was in our garden this morning. I watched it pull a long worm from the dirt then fly away. 'Tis building a nest in our cherry tree. Every time our cat slinks outside to hunt, I think about the little birds trying to protect their eggs.

There are fewer pigs in the street this spring. Methinks the British have made meals of them! If all the pigs get eaten, I know not what will clean up the garbage that people throw from their windows.

For schoolwork, Mama has me read from our Bible. The print is small and many of the words are hard, but she says to keep reading anyway.

"It takes courage to learn, Hope. Someday you shall understand what the words mean."

Monday, the 23rd of March

Rain.

Faith and I amused ourselves by rolling a rubber ball back and forth in front of the hearth, then we played house with Ethan's tin soldiers. When she tired of that we played dominoes, though she did not understand the rules. (I let her move her pieces wherever she wanted.) After she tired of *that*, I let her crack an egg into a bowl to make a small ginger cake. While 'twas baking I let her hold my special doll. 'Tis from our English cousins and she is dressed as a fine London lady. (Faith peeked under the ruffled petticoats to see what she could see.) The doll has a feathered hat and tiny high-heeled shoes. I keep her in Mama's room, in our chest, so the cat will not play with the feathers.

Wednesday, the 1st of April

More rain.

A chimney sweep stood on our roof with his long brushes, scrubbing the bricks up and down. Oh, the muddy soot that fell into our hearth! Mama, Miss Sarah, and I mopped and swept for two hours, just to clean the mess.

Thursday, the 9th of April

In the middle of the night I woke to a wet sound, something I had not heard before. I listened, then knew it was coming from the floor in the corner. 'Twas too dark to see, but another sound told me all was well: purring, louder than ever. I wanted to look, but a candle would have woken everyone up so instead I lay under our cover, smiling to myself.

At daybreak, yes, 'twas kittens! Three of them. Faith's mouth dropped open at the sight of such tiny living creatures. When she reached out to touch them, Cat (that is what I call her now: Cat) lifted her front paw and batted her hand. One of her claws made a prick of blood by Faith's thumb. I thought surely my sister would wail, but she drew away from the kittens without a tear. I am glad she learned this lesson on her own.

Between chores, Miss Sarah keeps sitting down to rest. She says her back hurts.

Saturday, the 11th of April

No time to write. Miss Sarah is in Mother's room. She is very uncomfortable and has been moaning. The baby is sure to come soon, Mama says.

Half past eleven o'clock in the evening

No baby yet.

Because Major Quigley and his soldiers have all of their weapons and booty spread throughout the attic and much of our house, Faith has no other place to sleep save her trundle.

I tucked her in a few hours ago, but she would not settle down. 'Tis not her fault, for Mama and I are in and out of the room with fresh water and so forth. A lantern hanging from a high peg in the wall makes the room bright. When Miss Sarah cried out in pain, my little sister began to cry, too.

"Hush now." I pulled Faith into my lap. "Remember Cat and her kittens?"

Faith nodded her head up and down, the strings on her nightcap loose below her chin.

"Well," said I, "soon Miss Sarah shall have a baby of her own. But we must be ever so patient and still."

Two hours later

'Tis long past midnight. Major Quigley and his men are yet out at the taverns. At long last, Faith fell asleep.

I know not what to do about a baby being born. When Mama birthed Faith, 'twas out in the garden at the end of a hot summer day. One moment Mama was picking a melon, the next (it seemed) I was holding my tiny new sister. Her middle name, Strawberry, honors her red hair and that she was born near our strawberry patch.

Alas, my eyes blur from fatigue. The last time I stayed awake this late was when I was waiting up for Papa's return.

Sunday, the 12th of April

Such happy news — a wee little girl was born an hour ago to Miss Sarah.

I have made porridge and a pot of hot mint tea for us all. (We do not drink Major Quigley's English tea.) 'Tis not yet dawn, but at sunup I shall run to Hannie's for a fresh loaf of bread.

Dear me, how are we to get all our tarts baked today? Even though 'tis Sunday, Mama says we shan't rest, for we need the money. The soldiers are eating our cupboards bare. Soon our cellar shall be empty, too.

Noon

About the birth . . . Mama said, "Almost, Sarah . . . don't give up dear girl . . . 'twill be any moment."

Just then, the soldiers made a noisy

entrance into our house after their night out. I hurried to our bedroom door and leaned against it so they would not try to come in — at least I would try to stop them.

Miss Sarah groaned, but Mama said, "Hush, Sarah. We do not want those drunk men to disturb us . . . 'tis almost over now."

A moment later Miss Sarah took a deep breath and with a loud sigh her baby was born. 'Twas pink and wet. Mama quickly wrapped it tight and put the baby in Miss Sarah's arms. It cried not, but made funny faces as it tried to open its eyes and look at its mother.

Oh, bother . . . Major Quigley is calling me to find his pipe. He forgot he left it on the mantel. He must need it to scratch his fleas.

Wednesday, the 15th of April

A curious bit of news . . . This morning when I walked to Hannie's I saw Lucy there. She has run away from her home in Valley Forge because of a dreadful event. Her parents shaved her head! They did so when they learned Lucy had sold her hair to a wig maker who does business with the Redcoats. To make matters worse, Lucy had hidden her nine shillings in a hen's nest in their barn. But when a soldier sneaked in to steal eggs he also took her coins.

I wanted so much to ask if she'd seen my brother, but she did not want to chit and chat. She looks sad and pale. Scabs on her scalp are left over from the razor.

"When my hair grows down to my chin," she told me, looking down at her feet, "then I shall return to my family."

'Twas all she said to me. I want to be her friend, but she is embarrassed and wants only to help Hannie.

Before leaving, I asked Hannie if Polly ever comes in to buy bread.

"No," she said, "just her mother and sometimes those wee little brothers."

'Tis mean for me to think this, but Polly's parents have made her a prisoner just to keep us from seeing each other. And Lucy's parents have made her a prisoner, too, but for different reasons.

I hate this war. Our captured soldiers are not the only ones in prison.

Seven o'clock in the evening

During supper I told Mama about Lucy's troubles. She shook her head, but said naught. My thoughts turned to Polly. All I said was how horrible war is and I think this should be the last one on earth, ever, ever.

The room was quiet as Mama served our stew.

"Daughter," she said. "War is terrible, yes. But sometimes 'tis needed. When tyrants rule people with cruelties, polite words do not make them stop. This war is for a good cause: liberty and freedom."

This reminds me! Miss Sarah named her baby Patience Liberty Dean.

Before bed

I am sitting on the hearth with my back against the warm bricks. My fingers are stained blue because some moments ago Cat curled against my hand — purring — then by accident knocked over my jug of ink. While I wiped up the spill with a rag I scolded her. But she ignored me and returned to her kittens.

We wait for word from Papa or Ethan or even our Potter cousins in Valley Forge, but no word comes. In our bedtime prayers we plead with God to take care of our men and to take care of Washington's soldiers.

Three of us under this roof have names that say something:

Hope

Faith

Patience

But I am not patient. My faith is weak. And only at times do I feel hopeful.

Another day

Rain and more rain.

Sunday, the 26th of April

Church. Baby Patience slept on Miss Sarah's lap without a peep.

On our walk home we went the long way around two blocks, just to smell the new flowers and buds.

"How I love it when the dogwoods bloom," said Mother.

The mercury read forty-eight degrees when we walked in the back door.

Monday, the 4th of May

At Market I bought some neck-beef and greens to make a broth for supper. While there, I met a kindly Negro lady, also with a basket on her arm. Her hair was wrapped in a blue and red scarf.

We said hello, then she began speaking faster than anyone I know. In just a brief moment she told me she was a freed slave and works for a Philadelphia gentleman. His house is in the country at the edge of town. Just this morning he paid her two dollars in silver for the washing so she walked to Market, three miles. She was buying food to help our soldiers who have been locked up in the Walnut Street gaol. What she needed now was bread, but she had already spent her money.

Without thinking, I said, "We can help. I shall bring meat pies and bread and tarts."

Her smile showed off her white teeth. "Chile," she said, "you an angel."

I ran all the way home. The lady and I shall meet on the morrow. Her name is Miss Charlotte.

Tuesday, the 5th of May

Day is done. How tired am I.

Mama came with me to the gaol. We gathered six loaves of bread from Hannie (methinks *her* baby shall come any day now, too!), and we also brought assorted meat pies with berry tarts that we baked this morning. We met Miss Charlotte on the steps of the prison, then went in. 'Tis a gloomy, damp place with foul-smelling puddles on the floor. I stepped around them as best I could, but still my feet got wet. A British guard lifted the cloth on my basket to peek inside.

"Mmm," he said. He stuck his thumb into the crust of a chicken pie, brought it to his lips, then licked off the gravy. I wanted to slap his dirty hand, but held my temper. There were fleabites on his neck and his collar was stained gray. When he grinned at me I saw his upper teeth were missing.

Feeding our poor soldiers made me the happiest I have been in a very long while. They were ill-clad and suffered from wounds and bloody coughs. But oh, how they thanked us! Miss Charlotte wants to bring food again when she earns more money, and so do we. On our walk home we pointed to our house so she will know where to knock.

I pray Ethan is feeding Papa good hot broth and mayhap treating him to a fresh plum pie.

Wednesday, the 6th of May

From our window this afternoon, I saw Mr. Walker walking with his cane. He was slowly making his way along the cobbled street. Mother invited him in for tea. He is plump and jolly, but his wig fits him like a hat that is too big — methinks 'tis a funny thing for a wig maker to wear one that does not fit. When he bent over to shake hands with my little sister, the wig slipped over his eyes and landed on the floor.

Mr. Walker just picked it up, set it on his bald head, and smiled. Then he gave us good news. He said the Americans now have an alliance with France — a fleet of ships shall sail to our shores to help us! The treaty was arranged many weeks ago in Paris, by Benjamin Franklin.

At the name of Benjamin Franklin, I sat up straight. I have met him! 'Twas at Market when I was nine years of age. He was a pleasant old gentleman who paid me a silver shilling for a berry tart. I remember how he tucked the tart into the pocket of his waistcoat. He did not seem to mind that the juice stained the light blue satin purple.

I wonder what he wore to his meeting with the king of France. Mr. Walker said the king's name is Louis the Sixteenth.

Wednesday, the 13th of May

Miss Sarah, Mother, and I planted our garden today. We let Faith dig in the dirt with a stick because she is a big girl now. We set the cradle outside so Patience could see the pretty clouds and hear birds singing. Already she is four weeks old. Her little cap is made of lace with a yellow ribbon tied under her chin.

Mama said we are five ladies making the best of things.

We have held our breaths, waiting to hear if General Howe attacked Valley Forge. But so far, no reports.

Our neighbors at Market tell stories about the soldiers living under their roofs. We all agree: This winter has been one big party for the English. The officers drink so much wine and ale and they feast at so many banquets that they are like a group of plump ducks.

Secretly, this pleases us. If they are weak and bloated, mayhap they will wobble when they face our troops. We have heard that Washington's men are lean and ready for battle. They drill daily and are being taught to fight. And when the French arrive, our army shall be that much stronger.

This morning while we were eating hotcakes, a mouse ran from the cupboard toward our table. I lifted my feet so it would not run over my shoes. Cat was there with one quick swoop. I watched her carry her prize to her kittens. The last we saw of the mouse, 'twas still wiggling its tiny paws.

Friday, the 15th of May

A grand party today, but 'tis to honor General Howe. We went to the docks where people from every street stood watching. I looked for Polly, but saw only her papa with some other Tories — they waved small English flags is how I knew.

Along the river came a parade of British ships, small and large, handsome with flags and full sails. 'Twas quite a sight, but I wished the sailors on deck were our own, instead of Redcoats.

Late afternoon, near five o'clock, cannons began to fire. At the first explosion, every child along the wharf either screamed with excitement or began to cry. Faith turned her lip down and looked up at me, but no tears came. A moment later there was another cannon, then another. Nineteen in all. Still my sister did not cry, though she held tight to my skirt — she is a brave little Patriot!

Mama said 'twas a nineteen-gun salute. "To say *fare thee well* to the fattest commander in town."

A neighbor told us General Howe shall be sailing for England in a few days. Now we have more questions. Did he decide not to attack Valley Forge after all? Who will command the soldiers living in our city? We wonder most of all how long Major Quigley will be in our home.

Before bed

Mr. Walker ate supper with us this evening. Whilst he was carving his beef, one of the kittens climbed up his stocking and breeches. Its claws must have pricked because Mr. Walker's eyes grew big, but he did not drop his knife. When the kitten arrived in his lap and started purring, he looked down at it and smiled.

"Fancy that!" he said.

Later he told us about the Redcoats' new commander in chief. The man's name is Sir Henry Clinton.

Monday, the 18th of May

A warm, lovely day. We threw open all our windows to air the house. Since we no longer have a fence out back over which to hang our bedding, we fluffed our quilts and lay them in the sun. I swept the rooms, stairs, even the attic (as best I could). 'Twas such a clutter from Major Quigley I could only find a small path through the booty. Mama says that if he leaves we shall scrub every inch with lye. Fleas are in everything, and methinks I saw lice crawling over their pillows. Mouse droppings were on the windowsill.

Evening, ten o'clock

I walked with Faith down to the wharf where the breeze is cool — we were slow because her steps are so tiny. Redcoats were carrying trunks and parcels aboard ships. We stood with other Patriots, watching. We dare to hope this busyness means our enemies shall soon depart our city.

The day was pretty with sunshine. Clouds were high and white in the sky. The reason I am awake at this late hour is the fireworks. More loud pops, whistles, and explosions are lighting up the night to again honor General Howe. Mama said 'tis shameful how many Americans have turned coat just to be on the good side of our enemy.

By the next tide he shall sail from our shores. Hooray, I say.

I wanted to run outside and see the fireworks, but Mama said, "Enough is enough." Thus, here I sit by the hearth, watching the kittens wrestle with one another. Mr. Walker was so charmed by the one that climbed into his lap during supper that evening that we are giving it to him. He has named it Gray Boy. When 'tis old enough to be away from its mother, he shall take it home to his wig shoppe.

Friday, the 22nd of May

'Tis morning, seven o'clock. A surprise came just an hour ago . . . Lucy rapped on our door. She wore a cap over her head, tied with a blue bow so you could not see that she is bald.

"Mrs. Potter, ma'am?" she said. "Hannie is asking for you. Her time has come."

Mama put on a fresh apron and grabbed some clean white towels. When she saw that I, too, was putting on an apron she said, "Hope, thou must help watch over Faith and tend to our customers."

Alas, once again, here I sit. 'Twould be much more interesting to see another birthing, but I must obey Mama. Ah, a gentleman is here asking for a breakfast pie . . .

Noon

Mama returned just moments ago. "Hannie was delivered of a fine boy," she told me.

Now she and her husband have six little ones — Matthew Robert is the name of this new baby.

And do you know that before he was born, Hannie still rose early this morning to bake her bread? She gave Mama three loaves of dark rye.

Thursday, the 4th of June

More cannons! A boom rattled our windows early this morning. It so startled me, I dropped the bowl of cream I was carrying to Cat. She and her kittens licked up every drop, but still I was upset.

A lady customer told us 'twas a royal salute to mark the birthday of King George. Mama and Miss Sarah looked at each other and rolled their eyes. We have all had enough of King George.

Next day

Oh, my, but 'tis hot. The mercury stands at eighty-two degrees. The air is moist as steam. Our open windows just bring in a warm breeze, but at least the air moves.

A ship arrived from England full of goods

ordered some months ago by Loyalists. Faith and I were watching from the wharf when sailors began to unload. They pried open some of the crates because of foul odors. Nearly every cracker and the smoked beef were spoiled with maggots. Bolts of cloth were stained with mold. 'Twas four months and one week at sea with storms and flooded holds.

A Quaker man in a black hat and a black frock coat fainted on the dock. He, too, had been watching, but was overcome by the heat. A sailor poured a bucket of seawater over him and the fellow came to.

I took Faith home by way of Dock Creek, hoping we could get our feet wet, but it stunk with garbage! Instead we went to the inlet where Polly and I used to play during the summer. I untied my sister's shoes and took off her stockings, and together we waded up to our knees. Faith was so happy to be cool, she sat down in the water and splashed her arms. It seemed like such fun, I did the same. We splashed each other until our hair was dripping. Oh, how good it felt!

When Mama saw us come up the step with muddy hems, she scolded us not. Methinks she laughed, for when she turned away her shoulders were shaking.

Afternoon

In the alley around our corner a boy captured one of the loose pigs and fastened a harness to it. While Faith and I watched, the poor pig kept tossing its head, for it did not want to walk around in the heat like a pet dog. The boy said his mama shall cook it for dinner next Sunday.

Friday, the 12th of June

We ladies sat in our garden this evening to eat supper, for the house is hot from our oven. We had bowls of cool bean soup with chopped onions on top and sweet crackers. For dessert, sharp orange cheese that had come from the countryside.

But our peace was soon interrupted. We could hear Major Quigley stomp inside our house with some of his men. When he looked out the back door, he stared at us with anger.

"Where is our beef and gravy?" he asked.

Mama set her spoon down and turned toward the street. She pointed to the opening between houses. "There," she said. "The Indian Queen Café is that way, Major. My kitchen is closed."

I held my breath. How dare Mother be so

bold with an English officer? She seemed not the slightest bit afraid.

Through the doorway I could see soldiers. "Sir?" called one of them.

Major Quigley turned to answer. There was a clatter of bayonets, then they hurried out of the house. We could hear shouts coming from the street. When our front door slammed I looked at Mama. Her hands were in her lap, but they were shaking.

Now I know that being brave does not mean you are not afraid.

Sunday, the 14th of June

'Tis Flag Day, our second year in a row. We hung our Stars and Stripes on a stick by our front window. It looks pretty waving in the warm breeze. There are not as many this year, methinks because the enemy occupies our city. For some reason Mama is braver by the day and cares not what the Major might say.

Oh, today is also her birthday. I baked a small pan of shortbread for her and we ate it after church with a bit of chocolate. Mr. Walker joined us and gave Mama a pretty blue ribbon for her hair. When he walked back to his house he carried Gray Boy in his left arm whilst leaning on his cane with the other.

Next day

Before breakfast I was rolling out dough on the table when Major Quigley came into the house with two of his soldiers. I curtsied in greeting, but returned to my task.

". . . but, those are the orders," he said to his men. "By Thursday the eighteenth of this month . . ."

My ears tickled to know more. *Orders for what?* thought I. Patiently I kept rolling out my pie crust and listened. Soon I was rewarded.

The Redcoats must march out of Philadelphia in three days! Mr. Walker came over to tell us they are afraid of the French fleet sailing up the Delaware. It may be many months before those ships arrive, but still there is much hurrying about.

Thursday, the 18th of June

Such grand news! We awoke this morning to the clomping of boots up the stairs and down the stairs — the soldiers were leaving! Mama and Miss Sarah jumped up from bed and quickly dressed. Mother told me to stay in the room with Faith and the baby, but still I covered my nightdress with my shawl lest any of the men should see me.

Through a crack in the door I watched Mama and Miss Sarah scoop plates and cups into their aprons, then bring them to our room. Carefully they laid them on the bed, and went out again. Soon Mrs. Krenberry's teapot was rescued, some silver candlesticks, and other treasures I had seen in the attic.

Every time Major Quigley went upstairs, Mother found something else to rescue from what he had just brought downstairs. We could hear the men talking. They shall be marching away from our port city, mayhap to New Jersey — it seems they are more afraid of fighting the French than the Patriots. Hooray for the French!

I have only a moment to write, for Mama is filling a bucket with boiling water. We are going upstairs to clean the filth those Englishmen left behind. At long last, they are gone — hooray, hooray!

Friday, the 19th of June

'Tis late, but I must put my thoughts down before I sleep.

Once again I am in my attic room. It took all afternoon to scrub. The lye and hot water made our hands raw, but 'twas the only way we could kill the vermin. Now my little bed is my own and so is my writing table under the window. Its pane is propped open for a night breeze, but oh how the heat lingers. I can see over the dark rooftops to the river. A house nearby has a lantern in its upstairs window and someone is looking out. Another house has an open door with yellow light spilling into the street.

After I snuff out this candle, I shall join Mama, Miss Sarah, and the girls in our cellar. Its stone floor and stone walls make it the coolest spot to sleep. We have made one large mattress stuffed with straw. We do not even need a blanket.

Oh, there is so much to write, but I am too sleepy and 'tis too hot up here. I have news about Polly, also news about Ethan and my father.

We know not what the mercury says because Major Quigley stole our thermometer.

Morning, after baking

When we went next door with Miss Sarah to see her house, the stench coming through the open door made us all draw back.

'Tis ruined inside — cupboards torn apart, bed frames cut up for firewood, teacups smashed in the fireplace, rotting garbage strewn everywhere . . . oh, 'tis too much to describe.

Miss Sarah pulled her apron over her nose to cover the stink. She was distressed to tears.

"But there is so much to do," she cried.

"I know, my dear," said Mother. "But we shall all help. Soon 'twill be your lovely home once again."

Outside, we walked up one street and down another. Everywhere we looked, Patriots were busy with mops and hammers. Upon leaving, many of the Redcoats threw furniture, dishes, and clothes out windows, just to be mean. The streets are littered with broken china and chairs, paintings and cooking spoons.

Many homes are missing doors and windows, even roofs. 'Tis a discouraging sight. Mr. Walker told us the British destroyed six hundred houses. He said there are many, many families loyal to the king who now are fleeing Philadelphia. They will hide because they are afraid of being tarred and feathered by angry Patriots — I wonder if Mama or Miss Sarah would punish Polly's parents this way.

All day, Americans who had fled the city last September began returning. Some by cart and horse, but most were walking, carrying their small children. It made me sad to hear the women crying for their lost homes.

I am proud of Mother for saving Mrs. Krenberry's beautiful teapot.

Later

Redcoats set a torch to the shipyard where Ethan worked. All the new American ships being built were burned. Methinks Ethan would be sick at heart to see this.

We also learned our beautiful Independence Hall is ruined inside. Redcoats who lodged there used every chair, table, and bench for firewood.

After supper

Dishes are done and once again we are in the garden. Mama says that she does not recall ever experiencing such a hot summer in her lifetime.

As for news ... General Washington is marching out of Valley Forge with our fresh American army! We know not where they are going, but Ethan sent this letter by messenger:

Dear Mother,

I write to tell you Papa is sitting beside me in the shade of a tree. Our feet are cooling in the stream. You will be pleased to know he has gained much strength in the past weeks and is eager to serve our new country. He says to please not worry because he shall be a baker for the troops, not a soldier.

Mother, Papa said I may enlist if I have your permission, so I will wait word here at General Wayne's encampment.

Your loving son, Ethan
P.S. Did you hear the French are coming to help us?

Mama says not what her answer shall be.

Miss Sarah received a letter from her husband, Mr. Dean, but she tucked it in her bosom after reading. We know only that he is well and eager to fight the war to its end.

Saturday, the 27th of June

We feel safer tonight. A troop of Continentals paraded into the city to help protect us. They were wearing brown hunting shirts and breeches, with hats turned up in three places. Each carried a musket and wore a white belt across the shoulder. Mr. Walker said this belt carries their bullets. Marching in front of the soldiers were boys playing drums and fifes. These boys looked proud and happy, though methinks it had been some time since they last combed their hair. Then came four horses pulling a fancy coach. Inside was General Benedict Arnold. His hand held on to the carriage door and he lifted his fingers as if to wave at those standing in the street. His servants rode behind in other coaches, but did not look at us.

Neighbors are saying Benedict Arnold shall take command as military governor and that he is a trusted friend of General Washington.

Sunday, the 28th of June

How nice 'twas to sit in church without seeing Hessians and those silly girls. We felt the summer's heat even inside our pews. I fanned myself with a folded handbill I tore off a streetlamp. On it is written QUIGLEY'S HEADQUARTERS, BREAD STREET.

How very happy we are that Quigley's Headquarters are no more.

After our closing hymn, the rector led us in a prayer for our soldiers in Monmouth. He said today they are fighting the Redcoats under the most brutal heat in memory.

Evening, half past seven

Once again I am in the attic, window open. Mosquitoes are such a bother! I can hear them buzz by my ears and neck. 'Tis so hot even Cat will not come up here but stays outside.

I forgot to write that many of those pretty German girls married their Hessian soldiers and some sailed to Europe. On the ships returning to England, five hundred American families joined the British soldiers. Five hundred!

Alas, I am sad to say Polly was among them.

Too soon my candle is low and this heat upstairs unbearable. I shall write on the morrow when I shan't need a flame.

Monday, the 29th of June

In the garden come evening, fireflies appear. My Chubby Strawberry tries to catch them by clapping her hands together, but they escape. Their tiny twinkling lights are here, then there. Even the kittens jump with their paws in the air, but they do not catch them. Cat lies on her side watching, but only blinks her yellow eyes. She, too, is hot and tired.

Baby Patience is two months and two weeks old. In the cradle she bends her knees and grabs her bare toes. Her smile makes us laugh. The sweet wee thing knows nothing of war or broken things or lost friends.

I do not talk to anyone about Polly. My heart hurts to think she is no longer here. 'Tis not easy to write . . .

Tuesday, the 30th of June

Major Quigley left behind some of his booty because 'twas too much for him to carry. He did not thank Mother for our roof or food, nor apologize for his mess. He walked out of the house without looking at us. 'Twas as if we were fleas on the floor.

"What do we need with all this?" Mama said. She shook her head as we looked about the parlor. Crates were stacked here and there.

We now have six quarts of Spanish olives, thirty-eight pounds of Parmesan cheese, a four-pound box of lemons, two dozen doilies, two dozen wineglasses, a dozen brandy goblets, a parcel of men's white stockings, and other trifles too numerous to count. When our neighbors return to the city, we shall invite them to share in Major Quigley's generosity.

When the Redcoats could no longer be seen anywhere in our streets, Mama and I walked to the gaol with pies for our prisoners. But a cheering crowd stopped us. Someone had opened the doors and our soldiers had been able to hobble out. Many have returned to their families.

Another thought

Miss Charlotte came to our door this morning to buy strawberry tarts. 'Tis her third visit.

"The gentleman favors your pies, ma'am," she said to Mother when we invited her in for tea. Sitting at our cozy table, she told us that she was born in Africa. When she was eight years old she came to America aboard a ship with her brother. I had many questions, but too soon she stood up to leave, saying the hour was late.

Mama gave her a parcel of cheese, some lemons, and a jar of olives. Outside by our corner, Miss Charlotte turned to wave good-bye. Her blue and red scarf was as colorful as a flag. A tear was in my eye because she had just told us about her daughter, my age. The girl had been sold to a plantation farther south.

This happened while Miss Charlotte was still a slave in Virginia. She has no money to search for her daughter or to buy her freedom.

Wednesday, the 1st of July

Oh, but 'tis hot! There is a warm dampness to the air, even at night. Flies swarm in the doorways and the mosquitoes are worse.

About Mama's letter to Ethan . . . she thought about things for more than a week. This morning Mama borrowed my jug of ink and quill to write a letter. Then she sent it by messenger to General Wayne's encampment.

She told Ethan that our home was safe and we were doing well. As he was fifteen years of age, he could choose for himself. He had her blessing.

Alas, methinks my brother by now is a soldier. We know not when we shall see him, but we are comforted by one thing: Papa is in the same camp and can look after him.

Saturday, the 4th of July

Bells throughout the city are ringing. 'Tis the second anniversary of our Declaration of Independence — this was the letter to King George saying we were tired of his laws and that we were no longer an English colony. The year 1776 was when we began using our new name, the United States of America.

Cannons have been exploding from different parts of the city. Stars and Stripes are everywhere I look, the most cheerful sight in our streets. If the Tories are around, I know not. The only British flag I saw was on a silversmith's shop. The smithy fled with his wife when neighbors tore down the flag and burned it on his doorstep. The wood of his door is scorched and someone drew on his outer walls with charcoal. The words are too impolite to write here.

Wednesday, the 8th of July

This morning I was thinking about Polly. The last time we saw each other, her father was hammering their shutters closed. She was standing in the street, looking up at the blank windows.

I ran to her. Her face was red from tears.

"Is it true?" I cried. "You are sailing for England?" I flung my arms around her neck and we clung to each other. I cared not that her father was shouting at me to go away.

"Polly, I shall always be your friend," I wept in her ear.

"And I yours," she said.

While her father was walking toward me I

reached in my apron pocket where I had put my five smooth stones.

"Here," said I, pressing them into her palm. "Now they are yours. To remind you to be brave."

Polly clutched the stones, just as her father put his hand on her shoulder. He saw not that I had given her something.

"Time for you to go, Hope," he said. His voice was gruff.

Polly and I looked at each other in tears, then I turned and ran home.

Evening, at my writing table

And so Polly has the stones Mr. Dean gave me so long ago. She knows the Bible story about David the shepherd boy who fought Goliath. All David had was five smooth stones from the river. With one stone in his sling and his faith in God, he slew a giant that was almost ten feet tall. He was brave.

I know not if I shall ever see Polly again, but I know she shall always be my friend. Mayhap a letter from her will someday find its way across the ocean into my hands.

I pray so.

After supper the two kittens found Mama's basket of yarn. They batted and rolled the balls across the floor before we saw what they were doing. 'Twas a mess, but I helped Mama wind the yarn up again. Methinks she was amused because she smiled whilst carrying the kittens outside.

Next day, noon

At Market this morning I saw Lucy. She was buying a leg of mutton and onions for Hannie's family. I was so surprised when she did not turn away, but instead smiled. Then she invited me to tea!

"Come at three o'clock," she said.

Now I must write quickly. Am about to take a pan of shortbread fresh from our oven. Oh, 'tis hot in this house, but Mama and I complain not. No longer are there any soldiers, nor Major Quigley. We feel free once again.

Evening

Such a grand afternoon. Lucy took my hand and led me outside to Hannie's tiny terrace. 'Twas cool in the deep shade of her tree. Hannie's little ones played in the garden, chasing one another among the rows of flowers.

Lucy's cheeks are now a healthy pink, and it appears she has been eating well. She even took off her cap. Soft brown hair covers her scalp in the same manner as baby Patience. Methinks Lucy is pretty. She loves living with Hannie and calls her "Auntie," as if she were her own niece.

Candle is low, must ready myself for bed. Oh, 'twas so sweet to chit and chat with a nice girl my age. Lucy is coming here tomorrow after chores. Then we shall walk along the wharves where 'twill be cooler. I want to show her where Polly and I used to wade in the shallows.

Sunday, the 12th of July

Church. Once again we are resting on this day, no baking. We use only a small fire to boil water for our tea.

Patience is now three months old. My sister loves to cover her with her little blanket as if she were the mother and Patience is her own baby. But 'tis too hot for a blanket. I showed

Faith how to fold it into a small pillow instead. At this, my sister stomped her feet and wailed. She wants to do what she wants to do.

Mama sat Faith on the footstool in the corner until she stopped her tantrum.

Monday, the 13th of July

Every day we clean something of Miss Sarah's house. Neighbors want to help, too, but are busy fixing their own ruined homes. We hired two newspaper boys to shovel out the filth in the cellar. Next we shall scrub it with lye and scalding water. Miss Sarah will need a carpenter to repair her cupboards, also to replace the floorboard where the soldiers cut a hole.

I am happy Miss Sarah and Patience are still living with us.

Thursday, the 16th of July

Today my Chubby Strawberry is two years old. Her curly red hair is too short to plait, but I tied a white bow by her ear. She was so pleased when I let her play with my doll all morning.

Then at noon, Lucy brought over a cake she had baked herself, chocolate with chocolate icing. Faith ate her portion with a large soup spoon, smearing chocolate all over her face. Whilst Mama cleaned my sister's cheeks with a damp cloth, a boy came to our door with a letter.

Miss Sarah thanked him with a little plum tart. "'Tis for you, Nan," she said to Mother.

Mama sat down to read. When she was done, she smiled and handed the letter to me.

"Here, Hope. 'Tis from your brother."

Ethan's handwriting was wobbly and the

ink was smeared in places, but I could understand most of it.

> *Dear Family,*
> *We march on the morrow for* . . . (here I could not make out the name). *Father sends his affections and says not to worry about us. Please tell Miss Sarah that Mr. Dean has been promoted to* . . . (again, the word was blurred) *and that we are all well.*
>
> *Your loving brother and son,*
> *Private Ethan Kern Potter*

Before bed

I have been thinking about our three names again.

Hope

Faith

Patience

At last I feel hopeful. The Redcoats are out of our city and soon I shall be able to go back to school. I am hopeful as well for my new friend, Lucy. Hannie has invited her to live with them, to help with the little children and to learn the trade of bread baking.

I have faith that our city shall once again be lovely and safe.

And whilst waiting for Papa and Ethan to return home, I shall try hard to be patient.

Life in America
in 1778

Historical Note

On December 19, 1777, General George Washington took his army to Valley Forge. While the enemy enjoyed plush living arrangements about eighteen miles away in Philadelphia, the Patriots camped through the cold winter in tents and crude log huts.

George Washington at Valley Forge

Ten days after General Howe evacuated Philadelphia in June 1778, Admiral the Comte d'Estaing's fleet arrived from France, just missing the chance to defeat the British at sea. The war continued to rage for three more years. On September 15, 1781, the French fleet

The surrender at Yorktown

was able to force British ships from Chesapeake Bay, leading to the Redcoats' surrender at Yorktown the next month. Not until a year later — November 30, 1782 — did the Americans and British finally sign a peace treaty in Paris.

Signing the Treaty of Paris

Meanwhile, American General Benedict Arnold had taken command of Philadelphia. He began to brood over what he thought was his country's ingratitude for his services and eventually conspired with the Redcoats in revenge. As a result, Benedict Arnold became the most famous traitor in United States history.

Benedict Arnold

About the Author

Kristiana Gregory enjoyed finishing Book Three of Hope's diary, the sequel to *Five Smooth Stones* and *We Are Patriots*. "I received lots of mail from young readers, wanting to know more about Hope and asking for her journals to end happily. I do hope they enjoy Book Three but also hope they understand that, when describing history, not all stories have perfect endings." She loves writing about Colonial America because several of her ancestors served in General Washington's army. Her other Colonial America title, set in 1777–1778, is *The Winter of Red Snow: The*

Revolutionary War Diary of Abigail Jane Stewart, which was made into an HBO Dear America movie.

Also on HBO was Kristiana Gregory's Royal Diary, *Cleopatra VII: Daughter of the Nile*. Her other Dear America titles are *Across the Wide and Lonesome Prairie: The Oregon Trail Diary of Hattie Campbell*; *The Great Railroad Race: The Diary of Libby West*; and *Seeds of Hope: The Gold Rush Diary of Susanna Fairchild*. She also is the author of Scholastic's Prairie River series and the Royal Diary, *Eleanor, Crown Jewel of Aquitaine*.

Kristiana Gregory's first historical novel, *Jenny of the Tetons*, won the 1989 Golden Kite Award from the Society of Children's Book Writers. In 1993, *Earthquake at Dawn* won the California Book Award for Juvenile Literature for ages 11–16. *The Stowaway:*

A Tale of California Pirates was voted a Best Children's Book of 1995 by *Parents'* magazine. She and her husband live in Boise, Idaho.

Acknowledgments

Grateful acknowledgment is made for permission to reprint the following:

Cover portrait by Glenn Harrington

Page 99: General Washington at Valley Forge, *Washington and Lafayette at Valley Forge*, Bettman/Corbis, New York.

Page 100: Surrender at Yorktown, engraving by Illman Bros., after the painting by Armand Dumaresq, LC-USZ62-5847. Courtesy of Library of Congress.

Page 101: Signing the Treaty of Paris, Culver Pictures, New York.

Page 102: Benedict Arnold, Hulton Archive, Getty Images, Inc., New York.

Other books in the My America series

Corey's Underground Railroad Diaries
by Sharon Dennis Wyeth

Elizabeth's Jamestown Colony Diaries
by Patricia Hermes

Hope's Revolutionary War Diaries
by Kristiana Gregory

Joshua's Oregon Trail Diaries
by Patricia Hermes

Meg's Prairie Diaries
by Kate McMullan

Sofia's Immigrant Diaries
by Kathryn Lasky

Virginia's Civil War Diaries
by Mary Pope Osborne

While the events described and some of the characters in this
book may be based on actual historical events and real people,
Hope Penny Potter is a fictional character, created by the author,
and her diary is a work of fiction.

Library of Congress Cataloging-in-Publication Data

Gregory, Kristiana.
When freedom comes / by Kristiana Gregory.
p.   cm. — (My America) (Hope's Revolutionary War diary; bk. 3)
ISBN 0-439-37053-1; 0-439-37054-X (pbk.)
I. Title.   II. Series.
[Fic] 21   20030544465
CIP AC

10 9 8 7 6 5 4 3 2 1   04 05 06 07 08

The display type was set in Nicolas Cochin.
The text type was set in Goudy.
Photo research by Amla Sanghvi
Book design by Elizabeth B. Parisi

Printed in the U.S.A.   23
First edition, May 2004